To

Camila,

MERRY CHRISTMAS!

Love from

....

Gingerbread Town

Camila sees a present
wrapped up neatly with a bow.
The label has a name,
and the wrapping seems to glow.

"This present is for me!" cries Camila,
with the biggest grin.

Camila opens it to look inside,
and suddenly falls in!

Camila's in the frosty woods,
looking at blue skies.
To find a world inside a box
is such a big surprise!

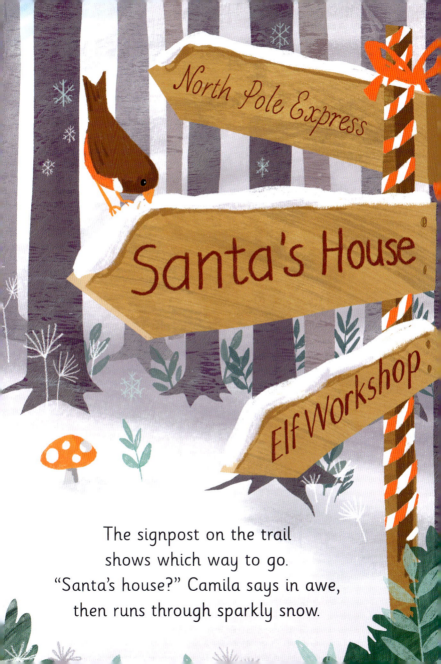

North Pole Express

Santa's House

Elf Workshop

The signpost on the trail
shows which way to go.
"Santa's house?" Camila says in awe,
then runs through sparkly snow.

Camila spots a village
and a family up ahead.
Camila gasps and can't believe,
they're made of gingerbread!

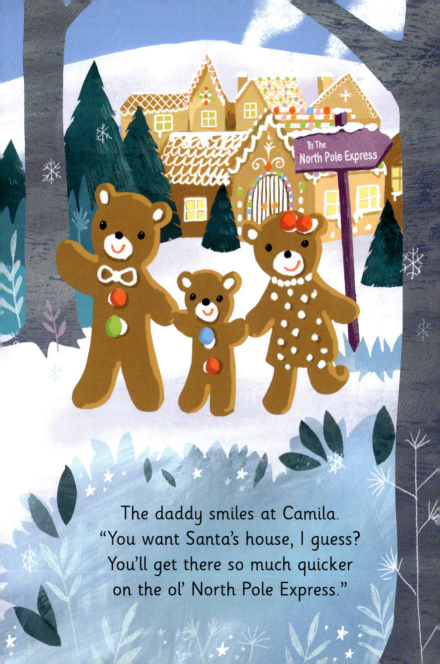

The daddy smiles at Camila.
"You want Santa's house, I guess?
You'll get there so much quicker
on the ol' North Pole Express."

Camila's at the station
and spots a little elf.
The elf exclaims, "I'm off to see
Santa Claus, himself."

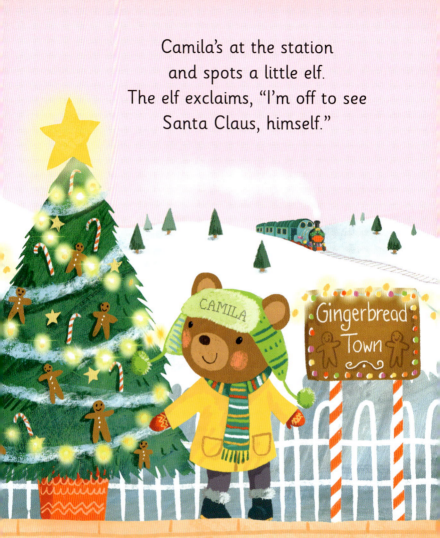

Camila is excited.
"Yes, I'm off to see him too!
But I'm not sure which way to go.
Can I come along with you?"

They hear a distant chugging sound,
then see the train appear.
The elf says, "Camila, this is it!
The North Pole Express is here!"

A small penguin conductor
brings the steam train to a stop.
"All aboard!" he shouts to Camila.
"Come ride with me up top."

Camila has the perfect seat
and an even better view.
Snowy forests whiz on by,
while the chimney toots "choo-choo!"

They reach their destination.
Camila's face is full of cheer.
The penguin blows his whistle,
shouting, "Hooray! We are here!"

The elf takes Camila to a house.
Mrs. Claus greets them with glee.
"I'm so glad you are here at last.
Come in and sit with me!"

Santa's House

Camila sips hot chocolate,
and eats warm cookies from a plate.
The elf says, "Camila, we must go.
We really can't be late."

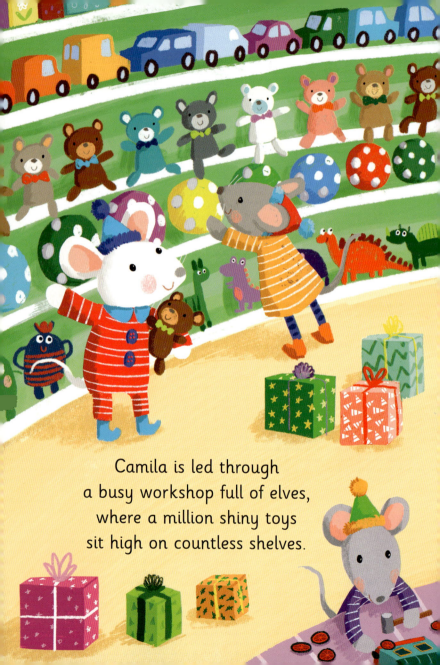

Camila is led through
a busy workshop full of elves,
where a million shiny toys
sit high on countless shelves.

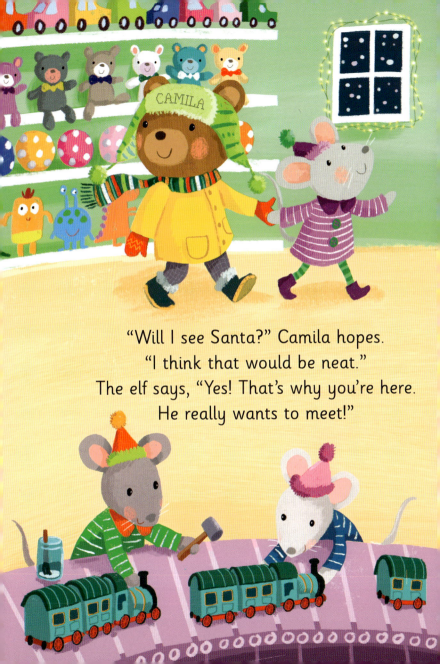

"Will I see Santa?" Camila hopes.
"I think that would be neat."
The elf says, "Yes! That's why you're here.
He really wants to meet!"

"Ho ho hello, Camila!
You've been sooo good this year.
That's why I left a magic gift—
so I could bring you here!"

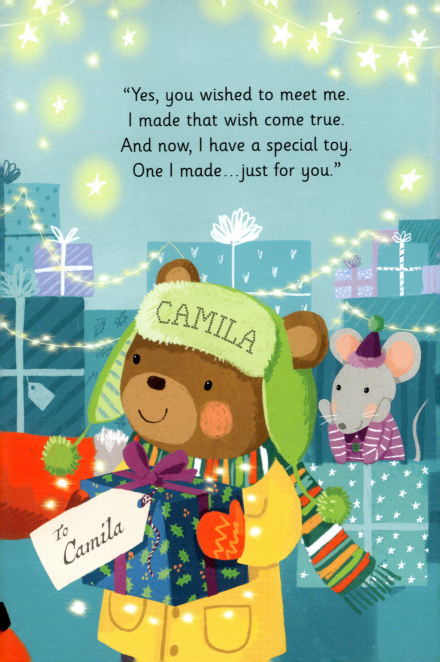

"Yes, you wished to meet me.
I made that wish come true.
And now, I have a special toy.
One I made...just for you."

Camila peeks inside the box.
What could this present be?
Santa magically disappears,
and Camila's by the tree.

The trip has been amazing,
a night Camila won't forget.
And in the box is Santa's gift:
a North Pole Express train set!

Camila, hop on board the
NORTH POLE EXPRESS!

Draw yourself and your friends
on the train to see Santa.

Written by J.D. Green
Illustrated by Joanne Partis
Designed by Ryan Dunn

Published by Put Me In The Story,
a publication of Sourcebooks.
P.O. Box 4410, Naperville, Illinois 60567-4410
(630) 536-1104
www.putmeinthestory.com

Date of Production: June 2022
Run Number: 5025359
Printed and bound in Italy (LG)
10 9 8 7 6 5 4 3 2 1

MIX
Paper from
responsible sources
FSC® C023419

Bestselling books starring your child!
www.putmeinthestory.com